Judge NOT!

Judge NOT!

retold and illustrated by

John Faulkner

Albert whitman & company chicago

©1968 BY ALBERT WHITMAN & COMPANY, CHICAGO. L.C. CATALOG CARD 68-22192
PUBLISHED SIMULTANEOUSLY IN CANADA BY GEORGE J. MCLEOD, LTD., TORONTO
LITHOGRAPHED IN THE UNITED STATES OF AMERICA

ABOUT how it began—

Tales told in the Middle East travel from storyteller to storyteller, from country to country. Sometimes they cross the ocean, as this story in one form did to be told in Detroit by an Armenian grandmother. An American scholar heard this story told of the Bedouins, while still another version is Turkish.

A good folktale is fun in itself. It takes on a special flavor if it gives a little taste of life in another time or place. In this retelling, a few words from the Middle East have been used. The true believer in Allah wants above all else to make the great pilgrimage, or haj, to Mecca. Then he will be a haji, or if he is old, a haji baba, or pilgrim grandfather. Perhaps his friends will address him respectfully as efendi, or sir.

Here, then, is the story of an old man and a kadi, or local judge, and what befell them.

ONCE THERE WAS and there wasn't, as tales used to begin, a weaver named Ahmet. His silks were so beautiful that none finer could be found, even in Damascus.

Ahmet was an old man, and he had just one wish. He wanted to go as a pilgrim to the holy city of Mecca. There the prophet Mohammed had first taught about Allah, the one God.

"If Allah is willing," Ahmet told himself, "when the time comes this year I will go to Mecca."

Rising from his loom, he pulled his long robe about him and set his turban straight. He pushed his feet into his shoes, then he picked up a roll of deep blue silk. It had been ordered by the richest woman in the town.

Ahmet's way led him through the donkey market, and the sounds of buying and selling filled his ears. Women stood visiting with each other at the fountain. In a coffee house men sat and talked, but Ahmet did not join them. He hurried on.

At the garden gate, the rich woman's little servant girl greeted Ahmet. "Selamunaleykum," she said, which means "Peace be with you."

"Aleykumselam," he answered. "Here is the silk your mistress ordered."

"It's beautiful!" cried the girl. "I wish silk like this were for me."

The old man smiled and repeated what his grandfather had once told him: "If a dog's prayers were answered, bones would fall like rain from the sky."

The girl laughed and carried the silk into the courtyard. While he waited, Ahmet could hear the fountain splashing and enjoy the shade of an apricot tree. Soon the girl was back with the money for the silk.

Ahmet walked quickly. Back at his loom, he counted his coins and smiled. Yes, there was enough money for his journey, and a little left over.

From the minaret of the mosque came the call for evening prayer. Tucking his purse away, Ahmet hastened to join the men who were washing at the fountain before going to kneel on the prayer rugs in the mosque.

"Your beard is long," a friend said. "Are you
going to Mecca? If so, take care that you are not
robbed along the way."

That night Ahmet began to worry. Where could he safely leave the money he would not need for his pilgrimage? He thought and thought. At last he knew what to do. Rising and slipping on his shoes, he went to the judge's house.

"Selamunaleykum!" Ahmet said, and when the judge had returned his greeting, he continued, "Everyone, efendi, knows what a wise and honest kadi you are. I have a small thing to ask of you."

The kadi was pleased with such praise. "Ask and if I can help you, I shall," he said.

"It is this," Ahmet explained. "I am going to Mecca. While I am gone I need a safe place to leave a little money."

"Aha," said the kadi, "I see your problem.
Leave the money with me. When you return, just
ask for it. I will give it to you immediately."

The judge stretched out his hand, and Ahmet
gave him the purse with the money. He was going
to ask for a note to show the kadi had his gold, but
if one cannot trust a friend—and that friend a judge
—who is to be trusted?

And so the old weaver set out on his pilgrimage. For forty days and forty nights he traveled. Sometimes he walked, sometimes he rode a bad-tempered camel. He was never alone, for many people were making the great pilgrimage to Mecca.

At a village close to Mecca the pilgrims stopped to prepare themselves to enter the holy city. Ahmet bathed, dressed himself in white, and had his head shaved. Then he was ready.

How long Ahmet had imagined what this day would be like! Now it had come. He was in Mecca at last! Ahead of him stood the great mosque and in its courtyard was the huge black stone, the ka'ba. A heavy cloth partly covered it.

Round and round the stone went the pilgrims,
saying their prayers. Ahmet touched the stone. For
the rest of his life he would have this moment to
remember.

With the greatest care Ahmet did all a good
pilgrim must do. Then he turned homeward, a haji,
or pilgrim, whom everyone would treat with honor.

Was the journey long and hard? Perhaps it was, but Ahmet's happiness made it seem short.

As he came near his own town, the old man made a plan. He would ask the kadi for his money and then he would begin his weaving. What lovely new patterns he would make—and all because he was now Haji Ahmet.

Next morning, after he had said his sunrise prayers, Ahmet hurried to the judge's house.

"Selamunaleykum!" he cried.

"Aleykumselam!" answered the judge. "Are you now indeed Haji Ahmet?"

The old man reported, "I have made the great pilgrimage to Mecca. I have prayed at the ka'ba."

"Splendid," said the kadi. "And now what can I do for you?"

"If it is not too much trouble," replied Ahmet, "I should like to have my money."

"Money? What money?" asked the kadi, frowning. "I cannot remember anything about money."

"But I left it with you before I went on my journey," protested Ahmet.

"You must be mistaken, old man," the kadi said. "Have you a paper to show that I am holding this money you say you left?"

"No, efendi, you said—"

"Then there is nothing to prove that there ever was any money. Perhaps you are trying to get something from me by a trick!"

The judge turned and called a servant and had him lead old Ahmet to the street door.

The weaver shook his head. "Vai, vai! I am an old man and it is the will of Allah. What can I do?"

Walking through the market, he did not see the ripe melons, the trays of figs, and the round, delicious peaches.

He moved slowly along, his head bowed.

"Selamunaleykum!" someone called to him.

"What is wrong, haji baba?"

It was the little servant girl. Not far away was her mistress, her face hidden by a veil.

The old weaver told his troubles. It was the will of Allah. He would have to work harder to make up his loss.

"Wait," said the little servant girl. "Grandmother says a little key can open a big door. Let me ask my mistress. She is as clever as she is rich."

That afternoon Ahmet sat at his loom. His shuttle moved back and forth, back and forth. A beautiful pattern grew as he worked.

A shadow crossed his loom and the old man turned. It was the little girl.

"Haji baba," she said. "My mistress has a plan. Tomorrow she will go to the kadi. When you see her pass, weave forty rows and then follow. As soon as you enter the kadi's house, ask for your money."

Old Ahmet did just as the girl said. When he saw the rich woman pass he was surprised to see her dressed for a journey. She carried a beautiful box, one that certainly contained her jewels.

Ahmet picked up his shuttle and counted as he wove forty rows. Then he, too, set off for the kadi's gate.

Inside, the judge was speaking to the rich woman. "You can trust me," he said. "While you go to join your husband I will be happy to keep your jewels safe. I hope that you have a safe journey and meet your husband soon."

Then the kadi caught sight of Ahmet and said, "Ah, here is Haji Ahmet. What can I do for you?"

"Efendi, I have come to ask for the money I left with you when I went to Mecca."

"Why, certainly," answered the kadi. "My servant will get it for you."

Turning to the rich woman, the judge said, "You see, here is this old weaver. He trusted me with his small bag of gold and now I return it without his even giving me a paper for it."

As the servant handed Ahmet the bag, the little girl came rushing in, out of breath.

"Oh, mistress!" she cried. "Such good news! The master has returned sooner than he was expected. You will not have to go to meet him."

The mistress took up her jewel box. As she did so, the little servant girl began to dance. All around the room she went. A moment later, old Ahmet, with his precious bag held tight, danced after her.

Round and round danced the old man and the little girl. And suddenly the kadi jumped up, clicked his heels, and joined the dance.

The rich woman's eyes were round with amazement. "I know why my servant dances," she said. "The master is home. I know why Haji Ahmet dances. He has his gold. But, kadi, why do you dance?"

"I've been a judge for forty years," answered the kadi, "and never before have I met a woman more clever than this!"

and so ends our tale!